# Mom at Work

Here is my mom.

She is driving.

Here is my mom.

She is reading.

Here is my mom.

She is writing.

Here is my mom.

She is eating.

Here is my mom.

She is typing.

Here is my mom.

She is talking.

Here is my mom.

She is smiling.

Here is my mom.

She is home.